Thankfulness Is Awesomeness

by Tina Gallo

Ready-to-Read

Simon Spotlight

New York   London   Toronto   Sydney   New Delhi

SIMON SPOTLIGHT
An imprint of Simon & Schuster Children's Publishing Division
1230 Avenue of the Americas, New York, New York 10020
This Simon Spotlight edition September 2016

For information about special discounts for bulk purchases, please contact
Simon & Schuster Special Sales at 1-866-506-1949 or business@simonandschuster.com.
Manufactured in the United States of America 0816 LAK
2 4 6 8 10 9 7 5 3 1
ISBN 978-1-4814-6819-0 (pbk)
ISBN 978-1-4814-6820-6 (hc)
ISBN 978-1-4814-6821-3 (eBook)

The holidays are quickly approaching, and everyone is happy.
Except for Po.

"I need to make a lot of gifts," Po tells Master Shifu. "There isn't enough time to make gifts for everyone, plus practice my kung fu . . . and naps . . . and six meals a day . . . I've got to tell you, I feel a little overwhelmed."

"You are concentrating on the wrong things, Po," Master Shifu tells him. "The holidays are a wonderful time because they remind you to think about everything you are thankful for. Make a list of all the good things in your life, and I guarantee you will not feel so overwhelmed."

Po likes this idea. "What is good in my life?" he says aloud. "My devastating good looks? My dazzling wit and hilarious sense of humor? Too obvious! Wait! I've got it! Kung fu!"

Kung fu makes me feel strong and powerful, Po thinks. And I am thankful for it because it helps me keep the Valley of Peace safe.

Po goes back to Master Shifu.
"*Skadoosh!* I've got it. I'm thankful for kung fu," he tells him.
"Well, that's a start," Shifu says.
"But you need to reflect a little bit more. What really makes your life special? What makes you happy?"

"Hmm. Let me get back to you on that," Po says.

Po decides to make a list of things that make him happy. "What makes me happy?" he says out loud.

"It's hard to think when I'm so hungry. Some of my dad's noodles would be good right now. And some dumplings. Polished off with a bean bun or two. Or three. *Yes!*"

Po writes down all his favorite foods on his list. Then he decides to visit his dad in his noodle shop and grab a bite to eat.

Po goes to Mr. Ping's noodle shop for a quick bite. Mr. Ping greets him with a big smile—and a steaming hot plate of noodles.

"Hello, son," Mr. Ping says. "Are you hungry? Ha, ha, ha! Silly question, right? Here are some noodles for you."

Po hugs his dad and eats the noodles happily. *I'm thankful for my dad,* he thinks. *He's awesome. And I'm thankful for noodles! Noodles are awesome, too!*

On the way back to the Jade Palace, Po runs into Tigress. "Hey, Tigress, what's up?" Po asks. "Do you feel like having some dumplings with me?" Tigress shakes her head. "Didn't I just see you leaving the noodle shop?"

"You did," Po says. "What's your point?"

Tigress sighs. "The point is, Po,
you need to stay in shape! Less
dumplings, more kung fu! Come on.
Train with me."

Tigress strikes a kung fu pose. Po
joins her.

I'm really thankful for Tigress, too,
Po thinks. *She helps keep me in
tip-top kung fu form.*

A little later Po sees Monkey. "Hey, Monkey, what's up?" Po asks.

"I am!" Monkey says, balancing his body on his tail.

"Nice," Po tells him. "Do you feel like having some dumplings with me?"

"Maybe later," Monkey says.

"Okay," Po answers and starts to walk away.

"Hey, Po!" Monkey laughs. "It's later!" And he joins Po on his quest for dumplings. As they enjoy their snack, Po realizes he is thankful for Monkey, too.

He's a great jokester, like me, Po thinks. *And also a great friend.*

When Po sees Viper, he can't help
but smile.
"What are you grinning at, Po?"
Viper asks him.
"I'm grinning at you," Po tells
her. "I'm smiling because you're
always so happy! What's your
secret?"

"My friends are always close by, and today I'm feeling super strong," Viper says.

Po agrees. "You're definitely super strong! You can crush any bad guys with one plunk of your tail."

"See? What's not to be happy about?" Viper says with a grin.

I'm thankful that Viper is on my side, Po thinks.

As Po thinks about all of his friends, he can't stop grinning.

"Hey, Po, what's so funny?" Crane asks him.

"I'm just happy thinking about all my friends, and that includes you, buddy!" Po says. "I'm thankful for you!"

"You're smart and peace-loving," Po continues. "You're a 'think first, punch second' kind of guy. But when it's time to fight, you've always got my back. Plus you can fly! When we need you to get someplace fast— *boom!* You're already there!"

"Hmm. I guess I am pretty cool," Crane says.

Just then Mantis appears. "What are you guys talking about?" he asks.
"Mantis, my little buddy!" Po cries. "I am thankful for you!"
Mantis turns to Crane. "What's up with him?" Mantis asks.
Crane shrugs. "It's nice to be appreciated!" he says. "Go with it."

Mantis laughs. "Okay, Po," he says. "Tell me why you're thankful for me."

"You're soooo much stronger than you look," Po says. "Look at you! You're teeny, but super fast. And your acupuncture attack is sweet! I'm telling you, you're the man! You're the man-tis!"

Po goes back to the Jade Palace to find Master Shifu.
On his way there he thinks about his home.

I'm thankful for the Jade Palace, Po thinks. *There's no place in the world I'd rather live. It has cool sacred scrolls and statues and an awesome big shiny table where we eat every day . . . speaking of which, I could sure go for some more noodles right about now . . . it's almost time for meal number four.*

When he gets to the Jade Palace, Master Shifu is waiting for him. "Well, Po?" he asks. "What have you learned?"

"I've learned that I really do have a lot to be thankful for," Po answers.

"I'm thankful for my family. I'm thankful for my friends. I'm thankful for the Jade Palace— my awesome home."

"Anything else?" Shifu asks.

"I'm thankful that I am a Dragon Warrior and know the secrets of kung fu," Po says.

"And I'm thankful for dumplings! And noodles . . . and bean buns . . . and snow peas . . . did I mention dumplings?"

"That's wonderful, Po," Shifu says. "Now, remember, if you take time to think about your world, you will always find things to be thankful for."

Shifu looks at Po hopefully. "Is there anything or anyone else you are thankful for?"

"And last but not least, I am thankful for you, Master Shifu! You push me to do my best every day. I could never have become the Dragon Warrior without your guidance and, um, patience," Po says. "Thank you, Po," Master Shifu says. "It's about time you said it—I mean, I am most certainly thankful for you, too."

"Sweet!" Po says. "And what do you know? I don't feel overwhelmed anymore. I feel peaceful and happy and ready to make some gifts. Thankfulness is awesomeness!"

What are *you* thankful for?